MRS. PIG GETS CROSS

And Other Stories

Mary Rayner

E. P. DUTTON   NEW YORK

for Bre Kerwin,
whose letter asking me to write back had no address

The following chapters in *Mrs. Pig Gets Cross* first appeared
in *Cricket* magazine as follows:

"Mrs. Pig Gets Cross" was in the February 1979 issue
under the title "Mrs. Pig Gives Up."

"Father Pig Sleeps On" was in the December 1983 issue
under the title "The Pig Family Again."

"The Potato Patch" was in the September 1978 issue
under the title "Two Piglets in the Potato Patch."

"Lettuce Is Too Flat" was in the November 1983 issue.

Library of Congress Cataloging-in-Publication Data
Rayner, Mary.
    Mrs. Pig gets cross and other stories.
    Summary: Life in the busy Pig household is always
eventful as Father, Mother, and their ten children
have a big party, struggle against bad moods, and all
end up in the same bed one night.
    [1. Pigs—Fiction.   2. Family life—Fiction]
    I. Title.   II. Title: Mistress Pig gets cross and other
stories.
PZ7.R2315Mj 1986   [E]   86-13433
ISBN 0-525-44280-4

Published in the United States 1987
by E. P. Dutton, 2 Park Avenue, New York, N.Y. 10016

Originally published in Great Britain 1986
by William Collins Sons & Co Ltd, 8 Grafton Street, London W1X 3LA

Printed in Hong Kong by South China Printing Co. OBE First Edition
ISBN 0-525-44280-4   10 9 8 7 6 5 4 3 2 1

Mrs. Pig Gets Cross   4

Wicked William   13

Father Pig Sleeps On   20

The Potato Patch   27

Lettuce is Too Flat   33

Piglets and Pancakes   39

Bathtime for Garth Pig   53

Mrs. Pig
Gets Cross

There once lived a family of pigs. There were
Father Pig and Mother Pig, and then there were
ten piglets. The eldest was Sorrel Pig. Then came

Bryony, then Hilary, then Sarah, then Toby, then Cindy and William and Alun, and finally the two smallest, Benjamin and Garth.

One day Mrs. Pig was picking up the toys strewn all over the kitchen floor. She grunted angrily. She hated bending because she was so stout. After picking up several more toys, she straightened up, banged them down on the table, and said, "I am not going to do any more. You are the most untidy piglets I know. Your things can just *stay* lying about. I am too tired to do it for you."

The ten piglets made a few halfhearted attempts to help. Some blocks were thrown into the block box. The railway that twined its way under and round and through the kitchen chairs was broken in pieces, but somehow it did not all get as far as its box.

When Mr. Pig came home after a late evening, he found the house looking messier than ever. He stepped over Garth Pig's tricycle in the hall, noted Toby's Lego rocket standing on the carpet beyond, glanced at the piles of coats, bags, papers and boots that lay on the stairs, and went into the living room. Mrs. Pig was lying on the sofa, reading a magazine. She said she was tired.

"Why can't you make the children clear up themselves?" grumbled Mr. Pig. "They should put away their own toys and clothes."

Mrs. Pig said sulkily that she had not felt up to getting them to do it. Then she and Mr. Pig began to argue about whose turn it was to make the tea, and in the end they went to bed without any. Father Pig was so put out that he forgot to lock the front door.

Halfway through the night, when the house was in darkness, a foxy-looking fellow came sneaking up the street. It was a burglar. He tried all the doors until he came to Mr. and Mrs. Pig's house. Their door opened easily.

The burglar crept in. There was a light on right

at the top of the stairs, but down in the hall it was pitch dark. He took a few steps forward and walked straight into Garth's tricycle. He banged his shin. *Eee* – He clapped a paw over his mouth to stop himself from crying out with pain. He tiptoed toward the stairs.

Crash! He stumbled over Toby's rocket. On he went. *Blap!* He trod on William's boot lying on the bottom step. He got up and began to creep up the stairs. Oops! Sarah's school bag strap caught his foot and nearly sent him flying. He staggered on toward what he thought must be the grown-ups' room.

He opened the door. Both were asleep. He crept round the bed to the dressing table and silently, silently slid open the drawers. Mrs. Pig kept all *her* things exactly where they ought to be. The burglar emptied her jewelry into a little bag and then went over to the bedside table. He found Mr. Pig's wallet laid neatly beside his loose change, and took them both.

The noise of falling pieces of rocket had slightly wakened Mr. Pig. Now he stirred in his sleep and gave a grunt.

The burglar fled. He ran lightly down the first few stairs – and fell headlong over William's other boot, dropping everything as he somersaulted down. Picking himself up, he felt about for the bag and the wallet. Ah, something soft. No, William's sock. At last he found the bag. Empty. Everything had shot out as he fell. A faint thump seemed to come from overhead. Feverishly the burglar groped about for the jewels and the wallet; there wasn't time to hunt for the small change. He found several small knobbly things, which he hastily stuffed into the bag, and something squarish, which felt like a wallet. He took it and ran out of the house.

When he reached a streetlight, the burglar paused for breath. He took out the wallet to count the money. It wasn't a wallet at all. It was the holder for Sorrel's old bus pass, which she had left lying on the hall floor. He threw it down angrily. Then he opened the bag and emptied it into his paw.

Out came about twenty pieces of Lego toys! The burglar jumped up and down with rage and went home a sadder and a wiser fellow.

And in case you are thinking that this story tells you never to put your things away in their proper places, it does not. It says: Be careful not to make your mother and father so cross that they forget to bolt the doors.

Wicked William

William was the naughtiest little pig. When he was small, he had learned to climb out of his crib at an earlier age than any of the others, and as he grew bigger, when they all played games, it would be William who pretended to be the wicked one. If Alun and Toby were policemen, it would be William who was the bank robber. And if they all sat in the apple tree pretending it was a ship, it would be William who climbed the highest swaying branch to tie on a skull-and-crossbones flag and say he was a pirate.

Some mornings William went down to breakfast while Mrs. Pig was still dressing the two smallest piglets. She would come down to find all the cream gone and William halfway through his third bowl of cereal.

He could not help teasing his two little brothers, Benjamin and Garth. Once, when all the piglets were tucked up for the night, William

waited until Garth's eyes were closed and the only thing that showed that he was not quite asleep was the steady *suck, suck, suck,* as he sucked his blanket. Then William leaned over from his bunk and called down briskly, "Time to get up, Garth. It's morning time!"

And poor Garth had stumbled out of bed half asleep and gone down to his parents, saying, "It's not morning, is it? William says it's morning."

"Oh, the rascal," Mrs. Pig had said, smiling in spite of herself as she kissed Garth better and carried him upstairs again.

One morning William felt extra full of energy. He had been away from school with chicken pox but was now quite better. He had tied a hanky over his snout and was pretending to be a burglar.

"Can we play?" asked Benjamin and Garth.

"Oh all right," said William.

"Wait for me," said Garth, and he ran off to the bathroom.

"Do you want help?" asked William.

"No," shouted Garth. "I can go all by myself."

William began to stack pieces of paper on the top bunk. "This will be the money I steal," he said to Ben, "and the bunk beds can be the house. I shall climb in and tie you and Garth up, and leave you in the top attic while I escape. It will take all day for anyone to find you."

Had it been such a good idea to ask to play? Ben wondered. He stood hesitating, but just then a terrible squealing could be heard coming from the bathroom.

William and Benjamin ran toward the sound. It was Garth, crying and shouting and beating on the door. "I can't get out. I can't open it. It's locked."

Mother Pig came hurrying up from the
kitchen, wiping her wet trotters on a tea towel.
"Now what have you done to him?" she said,
cuffing William as he and Benjamin stood by the
door.

"Nothing," said William indignantly. "He's
locked himself in."

"It's all right, Garth," Mrs. Pig called. "We'll
soon have you out."

The squealing stopped, and they could hear a
tap running.

"Turn the tap off," shouted Mrs. Pig through
the keyhole.

"I can't, it's stuck." And Garth began to cry again.

Mrs. Pig looked worried. "How will we ever get him out?" she whispered. "There's only one little window, and the water will soon be everywhere."

"I can try and climb up to the window," said William. "I'm sure I can. I'm not too big to fit through it."

"Oh William, yes," said his mother, and they ran down to the back of the house.

Carefully William began to scale the upright drainpipe that led down the back wall. Water was beginning to stream out of the overflow pipe from the bath down onto the concrete path. Garth's face appeared, red and anxious, at the little window.

"It's all right," shouted
William, "I'm coming."

With a struggle he reached the point where a second pipe joined the main one. It sloped sideways up toward the bathroom. Slowly William inched his way along it, toward the little window. Mrs. Pig covered her eyes and held her breath. I'm sure he'll fall, she thought.

But not for nothing had William so often played at burglars. Within minutes he had reached the window. "Out of the way, Garth!" And he levered himself up onto the windowsill, and the two watching pigs below saw him disappear into the bathroom.

In no time the tap was off and the door was open again, and Garth was freed.

"You climbed just like a real burglar," said Garth admiringly.

William grinned behind his hanky.

"I'm sorry, Will," said their mother, bringing a bucket and mop to clear up all the water. "I thought you were teasing him again."

"When I grow up," said Garth, "I'm going to be a burglar."

Father Pig Sleeps On

Thump!

Benjamin Pig woke with a start. He had rolled out of bed. Leaving his nine brothers and sisters asleep in their bunks, he went stumbling down into his mother and father's room. Mrs. Pig turned over sleepily and lifted up the blankets for him. Benjamin climbed in, snuggled down beside her, and soon was fast asleep. Father Pig did not waken. *Snore-whew.*

In a few minutes Garth appeared at the bedroom door, rubbing his eyes and trailing his blanket. "Ben," he mumbled. "Where Ben?"

Mrs. Pig leaned over Ben and helped Garth into the bed. Then they all fell sound asleep.

Time passed, and the clock in the hall struck two – *ding, ding.* In the second bunk up, Alun was having a nightmare. He kicked and struggled in his dream, and woke William, who lay at the other end of his bed. William went down to find his mother. He scrambled over his two small brothers to be given a hug. Father Pig slept on. *Snore-whew*.

After half an hour, Alun's voice came from the doorway: "I've had a bad dream." He climbed onto the bed down by Father Pig's feet and squeezed himself in between his mother and father. Father Pig slept on. *Snore-whew*.

Mrs. Pig tried hard to get back to sleep. Then she dreamed that she was a toasted sandwich, very squashed and much too hot. She opened her eyes to see another of her piglets, pale in the dark.

"I can't sleep," said Sarah, ears drooping.

"Oh, all right," said Mrs. Pig crossly. "Get in."

Soon the door creaked open again, and it was Hilary who scrambled into bed, leaving the door wide.

Cindy and Toby, asleep in the third bunk, had been awakened by Hilary climbing down past them.

"I'm thirsty," said Toby.

"Me too," whispered Cindy. "Will you bring me a drink?"

Toby trotted downstairs and got a drink. He filled a mug for Cindy and was on his way back when he glanced into his parents' room. He saw William and Alun lying snug on each side of his mother, and at once wanted to be there too. He wriggled himself down between William and Mother Pig. Father Pig slept on. *Snore-whew.*

Upstairs, Cindy lay looking at the springs of the bunk above her and getting thirstier and thirstier. No Toby. She went down and looked in the bathroom, had a drink and then tiptoed into Mr. and Mrs. Pig's room. Seven piglets lay snug beside their mother and father.

Not wanting to be left out, Cindy climbed in. Father Pig slept on. *Snore-whew.*

Now only Sorrel and Bryony were left, in their top bunk. The clock struck four – *ding, ding, ding, ding* – and Bryony awoke. She leaned over, took one look at the empty bunks below, and shook Sorrel awake.

They both ran down and squeezed into the big
bed.

At last Father Pig woke up, it was such a
squash. He felt as if he were balancing on a
mountain ledge. He looked at his ten sleeping
children and felt too tired to carry them back up
to their own bunks. He leaned across, shook
Mrs. Pig's shoulder, and whispered, "Come with
me."

Mrs. Pig slipped out of bed, leaving the ten
piglets where they lay, and tiptoed upstairs after
Mr. Pig. With a satisfied grunt, he lowered
himself into the bottom bunk. Mrs. Pig settled
herself in the one above, and they fell asleep. For

the rest of the night, there was no sound from anyone – except Father Pig. *Snore-whew.*

Early next morning the piglets woke up. They had slept badly and sat up, looking round for their mother and father.

"Mummy!" they called. No reply.

"Daddy?"

Silence. Perhaps they shouldn't have come down in the night? Had Mr. and Mrs. Pig gone away and left them?

"Where have they gone?" they said. "What shall we do?"

Sorrel went down to look in the kitchen, but everything was bare and neat, and there were no friendly signs of boiling kettles or cereal on the table.

She came upstairs while the others gathered on the landing and looked with worried faces through the banisters. For a while they sat huddled together, uncertain of what to do next.

Then, from above, they heard a sort of throat-clearing, a deep sort of *ahem-ahem*. They knew what that sound was. It was Father Pig's usual noise when he got up to shave in the morning.

Bounding upstairs, they met their parents coming down from the top landing. "Out of the way now, piglets," said Mother Pig, but she was smiling. "We slept very well from four o'clock on – I don't suppose you did. But don't you dare all come down again, not ever!"

The Potato Patch

"This afternoon I have to do some gardening," said Father Pig one Sunday. He looked round the table at his children. "Who would like to help me?"

"We will," said Alun and William Pig.

"Right," said Mr. Pig, "you can help me with the digging. It is time to plant the potatoes."

It took a great many potatoes to keep the Pig family going for a year, and it was a large patch of ground that needed digging. Mr. Pig worked away, but very soon Alun and William were bored. They went over to watch their father drop some of the little seed potatoes into holes in the ground, but he told them to go back and dig their own patch. They walked slowly back.

"Wait a minute, William," said Alun. "I've got an idea." And he ran indoors and up to their room.

Alun had a shoe box in which he kept his collection: some shells, half an old dried-out squash that was cut into a face, three or four feathers, some string, a jumble of felt-tip pens

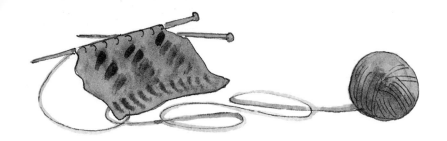

(most no longer in working order), some shriveled chestnuts, and twenty acorns. Alun picked out the acorns, the string, and the only pen that would write. Using the squash to hold them, he ran downstairs and fetched a piece of cardboard from the kitchen.

He wrote carefully on the cardboard: oaks. Then he spotted his mother's knitting, lying on her chair. He slipped out the two needles and took everything outside. He tied the string to one knitting needle and stuck it boldly in the newly-dug earth. Then he stretched the string out and tied it to the other needle. He spiked that one through the cardboard label and pushed it into the ground.

William bounded over to see what his brother was doing. Together they made a row of holes beside the string, just as their father had done for the potatoes, and dropped in the acorns one by one. Then they pushed back the earth to cover them. The felt-tip pen and the squash got buried too, but the piglets decided it didn't matter.

"I've got an even better idea," said William. "What about planting some bananas?" And he ran off to the kitchen. Soon he came back with a large bunch.

"I think they ought to be peeled, or they won't grow," said William. He dug a deep banana-shaped hole for the first one, but it seemed a shame to put the creamy fruit into the grubby earth. "I think half would grow just as well," he said, breaking it in two and popping one half into his mouth.

Alun dug the next hole. "I'm going to have a half too," he said.

And so they planted the whole row, eating a great many banana halves as they worked. They marked the banana row with a line of string and two stones, and sat back to admire their handiwork. Father Pig had his back to them and was still planting potatoes.

Shortly there appeared, panting up the garden path, the stout figure of Mother Pig. She was looking cross.

"Who has helped himself to all the bananas?" she demanded. "I was going to use them for supper."

William and Alun looked at each other uneasily.

"My knitting needles!" she exclaimed as she saw the first line of string. "You wicked piglets. What have you been up to?"

Alun pointed proudly to his label. "Now we will have acorns this winter as well as potatoes. We thought it would be nice. We've planted the bananas too."

Father Pig straightened up from his digging and groaned. "Oh dear, it would be years and years before the acorns are oak trees, and the winters here are much too cold for bananas. I will think twice before I ask you into the vegetable garden again."

Alun and William went sadly indoors. But a few weeks later, unnoticed among the potato plants, there appeared a seedling that grew two enormous leaves. Then it grew more leaves, bigger still. And soon every morning it was producing large butter yellow flowers, each one as big as a teacup.

By afternoon they had wilted, but the next morning there were more. The bees loved them. The great thick stem of the plant scrambled and ramped in and out of the potato plants. By late summer the flowers had turned into long, fat, delicious squash, and even Father Pig had to be pleased.

But I am afraid the felt-tip pen never grew at all.

Lettuce is Too Flat

One by one the piglets blinked and stirred. They began to get up and dress, but Benjamin Pig stayed asleep, a small hump under the plaid blanket, only his snout showing.

"Wake up, Ben!" shouted the other piglets. "You'll make us all late!"

Benjamin opened his eyes, but he felt cross and at odds with himself and everyone else. Why should he get up? Everything he did had to fit in with the others. He and Garth had to wait in the cold outside *their* school in the afternoons, he had to watch the programs on television that *they* liked, and he had to play the games that *they* chose.

Today he was going to do what *he* wanted.
When Mrs. Pig came upstairs to get him dressed,
he wouldn't put on his blue shirt and insisted on
a purple striped one. He shouted that his
trousers were too loose and took clean ones out
of the drawer, even though the others were
hardly worn. And he refused point-blank to put
on a sweater at all.

It was the same all day. When Garth was
picked up to play with friends, they asked if
Benjamin would like to come too, but he said no.
He stayed at home and played his own games
that morning, and at lunchtime the trouble
started all over again.

Mother Pig opened the fridge door and took out some beets.

"Don't want beets," said Benjamin.

Mrs. Pig tried again. "What about a nice carrot?"

"Don't want carrot."

She took a deep breath. "Perhaps some lettuce?"

"Lettuce is too flat," shouted Benjamin. "And I don't want any lunch at all." He threw his mug at the wall so that milk spilled everywhere.

"All right," said Mrs. Pig, her patience at an end. "No lunch." She cleared up the milk and brewed herself a cup of tea. Benjamin flung himself down on the floor and began to cry. Mother Pig bent down to cuddle him, but he pushed her away. He lay in a corner by himself and played with his favorite car.

When it was three o'clock and time to start out
to collect the other piglets from school, Benjamin
had begged a couple of cookies from his mother,
but that was all he had eaten. He refused to sit in
his stroller, and dawdled along after her so
slowly that they were late.

Sarah Pig was already out of the school gate
and came scurrying toward them. She took one
look at Benjamin's tear-stained face and the
empty stroller, and knew that there had been
trouble.

"Come on, Ben," said Mrs. Pig. "Let's find the
other piglets."

"No, don't want to."

Sarah was in a hurry for her after-school
snack. Catching her mother's eye across Ben's
head, she whispered, "Wait, Mum, let me try."
She bent down toward Ben.

"Hullo, Ben," she said.

Ben said nothing. He scowled at her.

"I don't want to collect the other piglets, do you, Ben?"

"Yes I do," said Benjamin.

"Let's go without them."

"No, don't want to."

"And when we get home, I don't want anything to eat at all," said Sarah. "I don't want Mum to make anything at all."

"I do," shouted Benjamin. "I want *loads* to eat."

"All right," said Sarah. "And now I think I'll sit in the stroller and have a ride home."

"No, you can't have it," said Benjamin, climbing in quickly. "It's mine."

Before he could change his mind, Mother Pig
had pushed him up to the school gate, gathered
up the others, and hurried home. And no one
had ever seen Benjamin eat so much.

Piglets and Pancakes

One day Mrs. Pig was trying to make the piglets' beds. She balanced unsteadily with her hind legs on the second bunk and struggled to reach the far side of the top one to tuck in the blankets.

"Bother these bunks," she muttered. As she spoke, she missed her footing and slipped. Grabbing at the blanket, she landed heavily on the floor, taking all the bedding with her.

"This is the last time I make these beds. Sorrel! Bryony! Where are you?"

Sorrel's and Bryony's faces appeared on the landing below, looking inquiringly.

"In the future you will make your own beds," said Mother Pig. "And call Sarah and Hilary and Cindy."

The faces turned sulky. "Why should we have to, when the boys don't?" asked Bryony. "It's not fair."

"Fair or not, I am not making them any longer."

Sorrel went upstairs grumbling. Mrs. Pig rounded up Hilary and Cindy and Sarah and sent them up too. In the top attic, the five girl piglets made their beds and then Sorrel said, "The boys ought to be made to do theirs."

"But they help Dad with the digging and things like that," said Cindy. "I think it's fair for us to do one kind of job and the boys to do another. Girls are good at some things and boys at others."

"Ooh, Cindy!" said Sorrel in a shocked voice. "You'll be saying next that boys are cleverer and stronger than girls."

"No, I didn't say that at all, I just know I'd rather make beds than dig."

"Well, I wouldn't," said Sorrel. "Or at least I'd like to be allowed to choose. Girls are as strong as boys any day."

"Oh no, they're not," said William, coming into the bedroom at that moment. "Prove it."

Sorrel was silent. Then she said, "All right, we'll have a sports day. Boys against girls. You wait and see. And we'll finish up with a tug of war, just to show you."

"Done," said William.

The girl piglets spent all morning planning the sports and writing out programs. There would be races round the garden, a sack race, an egg and spoon race, a jumping competition, a pancake race, and then the final tug of war. Mrs. Pig and Sorrel mixed a great bowl of batter and cooked lots of pancakes in readiness.

"What's a pancake race?" asked Garth.

"You each have a pan with a pancake, and you have to run along as fast as you can and toss the pancake up in the air so that it turns over and lands back in the pan on its other side," explained Sorrel.

Garth made a face. It did not sound very easy to him, but William was grinning a pigletish grin. He wasn't thinking about the pancake race, he was thinking about the tug of war.

At last everything was ready. "Father Pig will have to be the judge," they decided.

The first race was the running race. Father Pig stood at the side of the lawn with a handkerchief raised.

"Go!" he bellowed, and down came the handkerchief.

The piglets tore down the garden, turned sharply round the potato patch at the far end, and panted back to the winning post. William was first. He was by far the quickest, but when it came to being careful in the egg and spoon race, he was not so good.

This time it was Sarah who won, with Cindy and Toby in second place together.

The sack race ended in laughter. It began well enough, with all ten piglets leaping along in their sacks, but after about three leaps Garth fell over, and then Benjamin fell over him, and Sorrel jumped sideways into Bryony, and pretty soon Mother and Father Pig had to untangle a mountain of squealing sacks. Nobody won.

The jumping went on a long time, with the rope raised higher each round. Garth and Benjamin were out, of course, right at the beginning because of their short little legs, but the others battled it out. Finally the highest jump was made by Hilary.

"There you are!" chanted Sorrel, dancing up and down. "We're winning, I told you so!"

"Just you wait," said William. "We'll show you."

When it came to the pancake race, Mother Pig
lined them all up across the lawn with their
pans. "One, two, three, go!" she shouted.

Benjamin sat down and ate his. Garth hurled
his pancake into the air. It landed *kerflump*
across Toby's eyes. Blinded, Toby banged into
William, and they both fell headlong, their
pancakes tumbling out into the grass. Cindy
threw hers into the air and lunged to catch it.
There was a crash as her pan hit Hilary's, and
both pancakes landed on the ground.

Meanwhile, Bryony was doing well, catching hers neatly and keeping up a steady pace toward the winning post. Not far behind came Alun, having decided that one toss was enough, holding his pan straight out in front of him and running for dear life. Bryony turned to look over her shoulder and stumbled, so that Alun thundered past and reached the winning post inches in front of her.

"Hooray!" shouted all the boys.

"Ya, boo!" shouted all the girls.

"Shush," said Father Pig, adding up the score, while the smaller piglets crawled about on the grass, picking up bits of pancake and cramming them into their mouths.

"It's absolutely even," announced Mr. Pig. "Everything depends on the tug of war. Come on, Mum, we've both got to join in now."

Mrs. Pig rolled up her sleeves and took her place at one end of the rope with Sarah, Sorrel, Hilary, Bryony, and Cindy. Father Pig made all the boys take the other side. He stood back.

"Take the strain," he said. They pulled the rope straight, and he tied his white handkerchief round it above the center line on the grass.

"Heave!" he shouted, and ran round to the back of the boys' team.

Quickest off the mark, the girls yanked it a little to their side while Father Pig was running round to the back, but the boys soon recovered and pulled back again. The boys were using all their weight and strength. The girls dug their trotters into the soft grass and pulled for all they were worth. But it was no good; the boys were gaining. Slowly, inch by inch, the handkerchief was being pulled over to their side.

"Oh," gasped Mrs. Pig.

"Uh," grunted Mr. Pig.

"Heave," shouted Sorrel, and "Ee-ee," went
the five girl piglets and Mrs. Pig in one big pull.
Back came the handkerchief across the mark, and
now it was the boys who gave ground.

Then suddenly, Garth slipped on a piece of pancake on the grass, and his feet shot from under him. Over went the three piglets behind him like a row of ninepins, leaving only Mr. Pig and William upright. The rope yielded so suddenly that the girls fell over too, landing in a

heap on top of Mrs. Pig and bringing William
and Father Pig crashing down too.

"We've won!" shouted all the girls.

"No, *we've* won!" shouted the boys.

"Quiet, I'm the judge," said Father Pig, getting
to his feet and peeling bits of soggy batter off his
trousers. "Nobody's won, it's a tie. But it's
okay." He turned to Mrs. Pig, who was sitting
panting on the grass. "I'll make our bed from
now on, and the boys will each make theirs too."

Mrs. Pig put an arm round Sorrel and
whispered in her ear, "That's victory. And who
made the pancakes? You and I did!"

Bathtime for Garth Pig

Mrs. Pig had decided. No more evenings out; leaving the piglets was too dangerous. Instead, she would cheer herself up by asking everybody in. They would have a party, a party for all their friends, a grown-ups' party with wine and delicious food. And, she thought as she stood all by herself washing up, she would make the piglets help.

The ten piglets were very excited when she
suggested it. Mr. and Mrs. Pig made a long list
of all the friends they would ask, and all the next
week Mrs. Pig mixed and rolled and baked and
chopped to make ready the food. The piglets
helped. They stirred and licked and sloshed and
spilled, and then cleaned up and started again,
but it all got done in the end. The pantry was
filled with pies and flans, and the fridge with
jellies and mousses.

On the afternoon of the party, the piglets were
sent upstairs. "But I want you all down here,
washed and in your best clothes, to hand round

the potato chips and nuts when everybody comes. And please be on your best behavior and remember your manners," said Mrs. Pig.

Mr. Pig tried out records to see if they would do.

"You're not going to *dance*?" asked Benjamin Pig, staring at him in surprise.

William began to laugh.

"Go on upstairs," said Mr. Pig huffily.

Mrs. Pig counted out knives and plates into piles and put them on the table. Mr. Pig went upstairs to change.

The front doorbell rang. "Oh bother, they're early," said Mrs. Pig, wiping her trotters on her apron and snatching it off before she ran to the front door. "How lovely to see you, do come in," she said, leading the visitors into the living room. Then she ran back to the kitchen.

William and Alun and Garth came downstairs in their best clothes, not quite as clean as Mother Pig had hoped.

"Never mind that now," said Mrs. Pig, giving them each two plates to hold, one in either trotter, the only way of making sure that the food actually reached the living room.

The bell rang again. Sorrel Pig hurried to open

it and let in some more guests. There was a lady in a pink silk frock, and another in a lot of make-up and a spangled dress down to the floor. Sorrel could not remember where she had seen the spangly lady before, but she seemed to know her way about, and went straight to the living room.

The rest of the piglets came down, and more and more guests arrived. Father Pig came panting in. Very soon the room was filled with smoke and chatter.

Garth Pig felt like a sardine. If the walls of the room had been made of tin, he thought, they would bend outward, it was so full. A thin fog floated over everyone's head. Remarks which he could not understand bounced down from above. His eyes watered from the smoke. Bravely he hung on to his plate of peanuts and tried to squeeze through. Every now and then a grown-up would bend down and speak to him.

"Hullo, Benjamin, thank you."

"I'm Garth."

"What? Oh yes, sorry, I haven't seen you for a while, you've grown."

If I'd shrunk, thought Garth crossly, it might be worth pointing it out; but he said nothing. On and on it went, louder and louder, the talk and the laughter and now music as well. Over his head, frilled sleeves waved about, coated ones raised glasses. William pushed his way through toward him. "We're to go to bed," he shouted, "Mum says."

Garth was wedged between a long black skirt and a billowing flowery one, behind a low table. He could not move. William disappeared through the door into the hall. Garth ate several peanuts now that no one was looking, and peered round. He couldn't see any of his other brothers and sisters.

Someone had turned up Father Pig's record player, and music was thumping from the hall.

Garth squeezed between the black skirt and the flowery one and held up his plate of peanuts to the tall lady in the spangled dress. She leaned down, her beads dangling onto the plate.

"No thank you, I don't eat peanuts. But my, you've grown into a fine plump piglet!" And she gave his cheek a playful pinch.

"Ow," said Garth. He looked round for Alun
or Toby, but they seemed to have left the room.

"If you're looking for your brothers and
sisters," said the lady helpfully, "I think they've
gone up to bed."

She bent down toward him. She seemed to be
wearing a very strong perfume. Even through

the smoke, it made Garth's nose tingle in an odd way, and he could feel the little bristles down his back stand on end. But he remembered his manners like a good little piglet, and said nothing.

The lady put a wet nose in his ear. "I'll take you up if you like, help give you your bath. I think your mother and dad are busy."

Garth put down his plate and reached up to take her paw. She pushed a way through the crowd toward the hall, and they went up the stairs together.

The lady led him into the bathroom, put the plug in, and turned on the hot tap.

Steam filled the bathroom, but she didn't turn on the cold. Her sparkly dress was clinging to her, and her makeup was running down her nose. She began to hum a little song, and Garth gave a gasp. He had heard that tune before.

"Fried or boiled, baked or roast,
  Or minced with mushyrooms on toast?"
she sang.

In the meantime, upstairs in the bedroom with
no grown-ups about, the other nine piglets had
changed straight into their pajamas and nighties
without washing or cleaning their teeth.

Sorrel was climbing into the top bunk she shared with Bryony when she noticed Benjamin all by himself in the bottom one. "Where's Garth?" she asked.

"Still downstairs, I saw him," said William.

"Better go and get him," said Sorrel. "Come on, everyone," and they ran down the stairs.

On the first floor landing, in spite of the noise coming from below, they heard the tap running in the bathroom and saw steam coming out from under the door. They tried the handle but it was shut.

"Locked himself in again, I suppose," said William. "Push, everybody."

They leaned against the door and it burst open.

"There you are!" said Sorrel to Garth, glancing up in surprise at the visitor beside him, who was just reaching across to the tap. Then she noticed the feet just showing beneath the spangled skirt, standing on the bath mat.

Sorrel moved quickly. She slipped forward, and bending down, snatched the bath mat out from under those feet. With a howl of dismay, the lady in the spangled dress fell with an enormous splash into the boiling hot bath.

But the spangled dress protected her. Scrabbling wildly, she shot out of the water, and before the other piglets had realized what was happening, she had flung open the bathroom window and leaped to the ground below.

The piglets watched open-mouthed as the bedraggled figure hobbled away down the path, and the last they saw before the darkness swallowed her up was the glint of a sequin in the gloom. And she was not seen again for a very long time, but that is another story.